OLIVER LUM

and the

Prickly Plum

Written and illustrated by

Jane Preece

Published in UK in October 2021

Copyright © 2021 Jane Preece

ISBN: 9798488670839

For all the children who love reading my stories.

I wrote this following on from the success of my first book, 'Oliver Lum and the Bubblegum'.

Thank you to Bruce, my champion, for your love and support always. You are my hero.

Thanks also to my family, friends and all the amazing people, who have bought my books and encouraged me on this creative journey.

I hope that this book gives you as much pleasure as it gave me to write and illustrate.

Until the next adventure.

All my love

Jane

X

Oliver's mum made a good plum jam,

But she wanted to be the best...

To create a jam so exceptional,

Out jamming all the rest.

One day she heard a whisper,

About an exquisite tasting plum.

She knew she had to have it,

But how to get hold of some?

The prickly plum was most unique.

Impossible to get,

And as we speak,

Only one plum had ever been found...

In the deep dark jungle of Bundamound.

And the prickly plum fruit only grows...

On the vine that twists around the Paradise Rose.

Then Oliver's mum had a cunning plan!

She called to Oliver,

"Come, as quick as you can."

She shared the location of the prickly plum,

As she whispered her plan to Oliver Lum.

"Oliver Lum, Oliver Lum...
Please fetch me this
marvellous, prickly plum."

So, Oliver set off upon his quest.
There was no time for him to rest.
Armed with a bag of his favourite stuff...

Oliver hoped that he had enough.

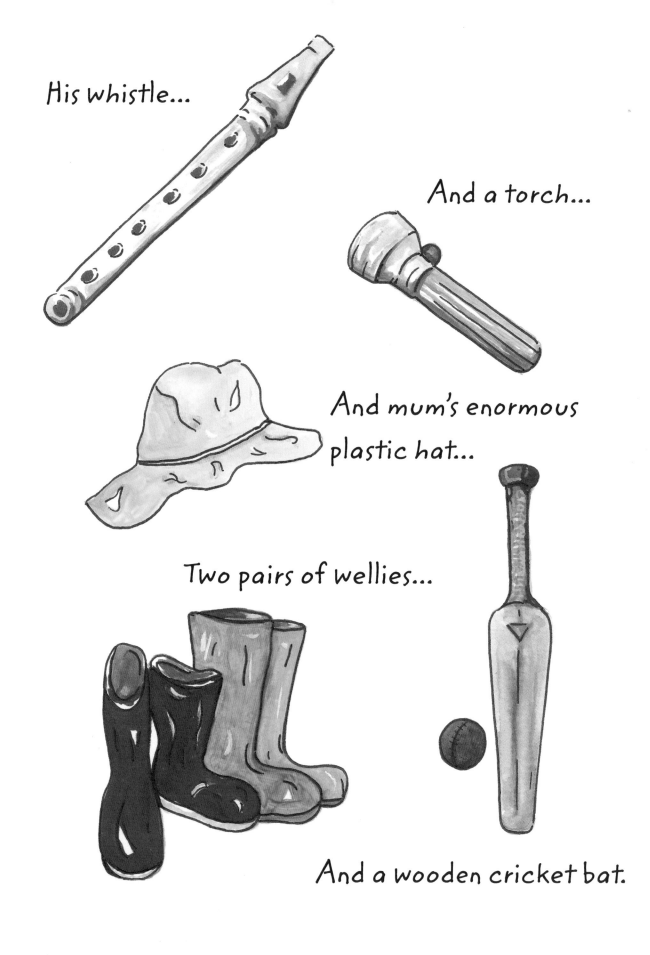

His whistle...

And a torch...

And mum's enormous plastic hat...

Two pairs of wellies...

And a wooden cricket bat.

He enlisted the help of Wayne, his best pal

And they borrowed a boat off another friend, Sal.

Across the ocean,
They sailed through the night.

Until the shoreline of Bundamound
Was clearly in their sight.

"Land Ahoy!" called Oliver.
"Anchor down!" yelled Wayne.
But as they dropped the anchor,
Dark clouds threatened rain.

"Ah ha" thought Oliver,
"Mum's plastic hat will do!"
"It's big enough for both of us,
Just right for me and you!"

When the thunder storm
had passed
And the sun shone bright
and hot,
Oliver grabbed his bag
of stuff
And said
"Let's see what's
what!"

They waded to the beach,

Wearing wellies from the bag,

But once they ventured on dry land,

They hit another snag.

A shroud of darkness fell on them,
As the jungle closed around.

Terrified,

All they could hear...

Was the eerie

jungle sound.

"Wooooooo"
"Ribbit ribbit"
"Squawk"
Eeeeek!
"Grrrrrrr"
"Sssssssssssss"

Without the sunlight guiding them,

The boys just could not see...

Then Oliver had a thought
And said,

"Ah ha, leave it to me!"

He found what he was looking for ...

"Hey presto,
We have light!"

He flicked the torch switch on
And its beam shone clear and bright.

A tropical tapestry lay ahead,

What a wonderful sight to see.

Flowers and insects, birds and plants,

Laced around every tree.

Treading ever so carefully,

Wayne and Oliver tiptoed through...

Past sleepy sloths and humming birds,
And flowers of every hue.

On and on they ventured,

Towards the place where the plum

vine grows,

When all of a sudden,

They stumbled upon,

The magnificent, Paradise Rose.

Winding around the rose,
Was a vine full of prickly plums.

But guarding the fruit so splendid,

Was a snake with slavering gums.

"You cannot take the fruit from here!"
The snake hissed and spat with glee.
"I guard this precious treasure
And it all belongs to me!"

Oliver reached inside his bag,

Because he knew he'd brought along...

His shiny, penny whistle,

To play a lilting song.

One by one,

They picked the plums,

Until they could take no more.

Creeping back the way they came,
Avoiding jungle roots,
They laughed aloud,
To know that they had bagged the tasty fruits.

Back on the boat,
Anchors away,
They tried to sail back home.

But alas, no wind, to fill the sails;
Stock-still in the salty foam.

"Ah ha" said Oliver Lum once more,

"I know what we could use."

"The cricket bat can be our oar...

Quick, no time to lose!"

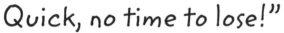

They rowed and rowed,

With all their might,

Until safely back on land.

And Oliver's mum

Held the precious fruit

Securely in her hand.

The jam was made
And sold out fast;
A sensation overnight!
Mum was beaming,
"Fame at last!"
Their future looked so bright.

But what is this in Oliver's bag,
Just starting to awake?

Oh no...

Oh dear...

A stowaway!

It has to be the...

SNAKE!

Printed in Great Britain
by Amazon